JENNIFER LOPEZ

A Real-Life Reader Biography

Valerie Menard

Mitchell Lane Publishers, Inc.
P.O. Box 619 • Bear, Delaware 19701

First Printing

Real-Life Reader Biographies

Selena	Robert Rodriguez	Mariah Carey	Rafael Palmeiro
Tommy Nuñez	Trent Dimas	Cristina Saralegui	Andres Galarraga
Oscar De La Hoya	Gloria Estefan	Jimmy Smits	Mary Joe Fernandez
Cesar Chavez	Chuck Norris	Sinbad	Paula Abdul
Vanessa Williams	Celine Dion	Mia Hamm	Sammy Sosa
Brandy	Michelle Kwan	Rosie O'Donnell	Shania Twain
Garth Brooks	Jeff Gordon	Mark McGwire	Salma Hayek
Sheila E.	Hollywood Hogan	Ricky Martin	Britney Spears
Arnold Schwarzenegger	**Jennifer Lopez**	Kobe Bryant	Derek Jeter
Steve Jobs	Sandra Bullock	Julia Roberts	Robin Williams
Jennifer Love Hewitt	Keri Russell	Sarah Michelle Gellar	Liv Tyler
Melissa Joan Hart	Drew Barrymore	Alicia Silverstone	Katie Holmes
Winona Ryder	Alyssa Milano	Freddie Prinze, Jr.	Enrique Iglesias
Christina Aguilera			

Library of Congress Cataloging-in-Publication Data
Menard, Valerie
        Jennier Lopez/Valerie Menard.
            p. cm. — (A real-life reader biography)
        Includes index.
        ISBN 1-58415-025-4
        1. Lopez, Jennifer, 1970- —Juvenile Literature. 2. Actors—United States—Biography—Juvenile litera-
ture. 3. Singers—United States—Biography—Juvenile literature. [1. Lopez, Jennifer, 1970- 2. Actors and
actresses. 3. Singers. 4. Women—Biography. 5. Puerto Ricans—Biography.] I. Title. II. Series.
PN2287.L634 M46 2000
791.43'028'092
[B]
                                                                                                    00-034923

ABOUT THE AUTHOR: Valerie Menard has been an editor for *Hispanic* magazine since the magazine moved to Austin, Texas, in July 1994. Before joining the magazine, she was a managing editor of a bilingual weekly, *La Prensa*. Valerie writes from a Latino perspective and as an advocate for Latino causes. She is the author of several biographies for children including *Oscar De La Hoya, Cristina Saralegui*, and *Salma Hayek* (Mitchell Lane) and the author of the newly published *Latinos: Traditional Celebrations, Modern Realities* (Marlowe).

PHOTO CREDITS: Cover: Reuters/Andrea Comas/Archive Photos; p. 4 Corbis/Mitch Gerber; p. 8 Corbis/ David Allen; p. 12 Globe Photos; p. 14 Rico Torres/Globe Photos; p. 16 Van Redin/Kobal Collection; p. 17 Merrick Morton/Kobal Collection; p. 21 Zade Rosenthal/Kobal Collection; p. 25 Lisa Rose/Globe Photos

ACKNOWLEDGMENTS: The following story has been thoroughly researched, and to the best of our knowledge, represents a true story. While every possible effort has been made to ensure accuracy, the publisher will not assume liability for damages caused by inaccuracies in the data, and makes no warranty on the accuracy of the information contained herein. This story has not been authorized by Jennifer Lopez or any of her representatives.

Table of Contents

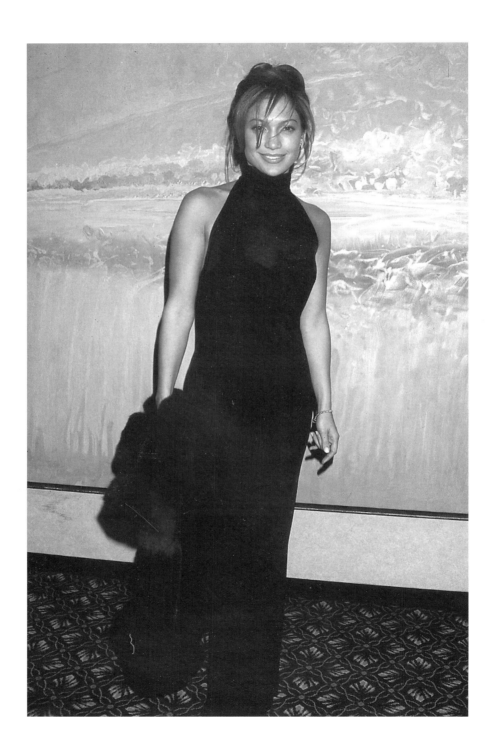

Chapter 1
Girl from the Bronx

Latinos captured a lot of headlines toward the end of the twentieth century, and one of the most prominent young Latinos of the nineties was Jennifer Lopez. In just four years, from the time she won her first major movie role in *Mi Familia* in 1995 to when she released her hugely successful first record, *On the 6*, in 1999, Jennifer has taken full advantage of every opportunity that has come her way. Her determination will help her continue to grow as one of America's biggest stars.

Jennifer knew early on that she not only wanted to be a star but that she

Jennifer has taken full advantage of every opportunity that has come her way.

didn't want to succeed in just one arena, like movies or music. She wanted to be like her idols who were successful in films and had top-selling records. "I want everything," she told a reporter for *Entertainment Weekly*. "I want family. I want to do good work. I want love. I want to be comfortable. I think of people like Cher and Bette Midler and Diana Ross and Barbara Streisand. That's always been the kind of career I've hoped to have. I want it all."

Her attraction to the entertainment industry was not unusual. For Jennifer, it was in her genes. Her mother, Guadalupe, and her sisters, Lynda and Leslie (Jennifer is the middle sister), all have musical abilities. Lynda is a disc jockey in New York and Leslie is a music teacher. "This is a musical family," wrote Martha Frankel in an article for *In Style* magazine. "All four women have wonderful, rich voices."

Jennifer is a native of New York City, born in the Bronx on July 24, 1970. Jennifer says she knew by the age of

> **Jennifer's attraction to the entertainment industry was in her genes.**

five, when she began to take dancing lessons, that she wanted to be an entertainer. She attended Holy Family School, a Catholic private school, where she studied dance, theater, and music, as well as regular classes.

She enjoyed acting and would pretend to be her favorite television characters for fun. One of the most popular shows in the seventies was *Charlie's Angels.* It was about three beautiful former policewomen, played by Kate Jackson, Farrah Fawcett, and Jaclyn Smith, who were hired by a rich man to work as private detectives. Jennifer, Leslie, and Lynda would act out the show, with each girl taking the part of her favorite character. Because of her light hair, Jennifer would play Farrah Fawcett's character, Jill.

Many children dream of fame, but reaching that goal can take years, sometimes even a lifetime. Jennifer showed that she was unique at a young age. By the time she turned sixteen, she had already acquired acting experience

Jennifer enjoyed acting and would pretend to be her favorite television characters for fun.

in small parts and television commercials. Her parents still hoped that she would give up acting and go to college to study law, but Jennifer had caught the acting bug and was not going to give up her dream. By the time she graduated from high school, she had decided to pursue her career as an entertainer. Her parents were upset at first—so much so that Jennifer left home and lived in a dance studio before getting an apartment with friends. Eventually, she was hired as a dancer

Jennifer's parents wanted her to give up acting to study law.

to perform in a European tour of the show *Golden Miracles of Broadway.*

Her parents always encouraged their children to be the best they could be. Her mother, Guadalupe, was born in

Puerto Rico but raised in New York. Her father, David, was born in the U.S. but is also of Puerto Rican descent. Today, her mother is a kindergarten teacher and her father is an insurance company computer specialist. Jennifer grew up in a middle class family, in the Bronx, a section of New York City that has a large Latino population. "It wasn't so much a bad neighborhood as one where you had to be careful," she remembers. "I have a lot of street smarts because of the neighborhood I grew up in."

Her first big break in show business came in 1990 when she was only twenty. Jennifer auditioned for and was cast in the Fox television show *In Living Color*. Like *The Simpsons, In Living Color* was one of the first hit television shows for the new network. It launched the careers of many comedic actors, including the show's creator, Keenan Wayans, his brothers, and Jim Carrey. Jennifer was part of the show's dance troupe, known as the Fly Girls. They would dance at the show's opening, middle, and end.

In 1990, Jennifer auditioned for and was cast in the Fox television show *In Living Color*, as a part of the show's dance troupe.

Jennifer beat out 2,000 girls who also auditioned.

Five years later, Jennifer scored her first breakthrough into movies when she was cast in the movie *Mi Familia* by director Gregory Nava. Though she had had a small role in the 1986 film *My Little Girl*, this was a much bigger part. Although not a starring role, she impressed director Francis Ford Coppola, who cast her in his film *Blood and Wine*. Her co-star in that movie was Jack Nicholson. She also won a role in the movie *Money Train*, with Woody Harrelson and Wesley Snipes. But *Mi Familia*, which told the story of a Mexican American family through several generations, proved the most important because she got to work with director Nava. That association would help her earn yet another breakthrough two years later, when she was cast in the starring role in the movie *Selena*.

```
· · · · · · · · · · · · · · · · · · · · · · · · ·
·                                               ·
·                                               ·
·            Chapter 2                          ·
·            Selena                             ·
·                                               ·
·                                               ·
· · · · · · · · · · · · · · · · · · · · · · · · ·
```

Selena Quintanilla Perez was only 23
years old when she died, but she had
already touched the Latino community
so deeply that she would never be
forgotten. The Mexican-American native
of Texas began singing Tejano tunes
when she was a child. Her talent and
charisma were so great that she
achieved success extremely early. But
her life ended on March 31, 1995, when
she was murdered by the president of
her fan club.

Latinos, especially in Texas, were
devastated by the loss of Selena. News
coverage of the event revealed that she

**Latinos
were
devastated
by the loss
of Selena
Quintanilla
Perez.**

had fans all over the country. Soon, people unfamiliar with her began to ask, "Who was Selena?" The story of Selena's life immediately caught the attention of Hollywood. It was time for the country to find out who she was. Selena's family asked director Gregory Nava to direct the film, and once he agreed, the next question was, "Who would play Selena?"

Jennifer performs in Selena

The chance to play Selena in a biopic (a movie about a real person's life) was a huge opportunity, especially for a Latina actress. Very few leading roles were offered to Latinos. Nava and Selena's father, Abraham Quintanilla, knew how important it was and how important this movie would be to the Latino community. They began a nationwide search for the actress who would play Selena. In cities like San Antonio, Los Angeles, and Chicago, Nava and his team issued open casting calls (when anyone, not just people with acting experience, can show up and audition for a part). It was through this process that Nava found the actress who would play Selena as a child, Becky Lee Meza. But finding the right girl to play Selena as a young woman was a bit more difficult, and it was getting political. The Latino community began to demand that the actress be Mexican-American, as Selena was. But in the end, Nava chose the actress with whom he had worked previously and who had some real film experience—Jennifer Lopez.

This was the kind of role about which any actress dreams. The story of Selena's life was triumphant as well as tragic. Jennifer was going to have to relate these aspects of her life as well as stay true to Selena's image. As a star, Selena was friendly, generous, and very

The part of Selena was the kind of role about which any actress dreams.

Jennifer wanted to capture Selena's personality down to the tiniest details.

humble. Jennifer was going to have to express these same characteristics. How well she accomplished these challenges could determine her future success as an actress. As an early incentive, Jennifer acquired something that was also a first for Latino actors—money. She became the first Latina to receive $1 million for a movie role.

The budget for *Selena* was $18 million, the most any Latino film had received until then. The budget allowed for actresses like Jennifer and actors like

Edward James Olmos, who played Abraham Quintanilla, and Jon Seda, who played Selena's husband, Chris Perez. But the pressure was on to make sure that the movie made money. But would audiences accept Jennifer as Selena? Jennifer also knew what was at stake. "This movie is the celebration of the life of an amazing person. Selena was someone who had not just tremendous talent but also a beautiful heart, and I think that's what her fans loved most about her," said Jennifer in *Hispanic* magazine. "I knew her memory was still fresh in their minds, so the most important thing for me was to get it right."

Jennifer has earned a reputation for her hard work. Director Oliver Stone complimented her work in his film *U-Turn*, saying, "She's there at seven in the morning, ready to rehearse, knows all her lines, and is fearless about doing her own stunts." Jennifer used this work ethic when preparing for the role as Selena. She took special care to recreate

Jennifer has earned a reputation for her hard work, which she lived up to in *Selena*.

Selena in every way. Once she was chosen for the part, she moved in with the Quintanillas and studied several family videos and home movies. "I didn't want to merely impersonate or caricature her," Jennifer told *Time* magazine. "I wanted to capture her personality, down to the tiniest details—even the way she rubbed her nose."

Jennifer in the thriller Ana-conda

Her hard work paid off. When *Selena* opened in May 1997, it earned the biggest opening day revenue for a Latino film, about $12 million. It surpassed even the studio's expectations. Jennifer also received high praise for her performance, and Latinos clearly found her performance as Selena convincing. The moment was powerful as well for the young actress. Remembering her first reaction to the film when she saw it herself, Jennifer told Jeffrey Ressner of *Time,* "I wanted to play her as the vibrant, alive person she was, instead of as a victim. I never broke down—until I saw the finished film. Then it just ripped me apart, and I sobbed nonstop for 40 minutes."

Many more movie roles for Jennifer would follow *Selena.* She co-starred in the thriller *Anaconda*, and in *Out of Sight.* She was also the voice of Azteca in the animated film *Antz.* But after *Selena,* her personal life would make its own U-turn and give Jennifer some valuable lessons.

Jennifer co-starred with George Clooney in Out of Sight.

Chapter 3
Jennifer in Love

Once *Selena* premiered, Jennifer would never again know privacy.

Jennifer Lopez seems fearless when it comes to how she lives her life. She's aggressive about her career, but also about love. Like many people who become famous, Jennifer's private life has become exposed to the public. Newspapers, television shows, and tabloids make many millions of dollars reporting on the lives of celebrities. Once *Selena* premiered, Jennifer would never again know privacy. But at the time, she was more concerned about planning her wedding.

Her choices in love have been wildly opposite, from a high school sweetheart to a hip-hop star with a police record. In some of the earliest interviews with Jennifer, she seemed completely devoted to her boyfriend at the time, David Cruz. They both went to the same high school. In a spring 1996 article in *Moderna* magazine, Christine Granados wrote, "The fast-paced life of Hollywood hasn't changed this *muchacha*. You won't see her party-hopping with the likes of Keanu Reeves or Brad Pitt. She is completely devoted to her high-school sweetheart, David Cruz. The precious little time she has away from work is saved for Cruz and her family."

But loving someone who has dreams of becoming a star isn't easy. For the partner of a celebrity, especially when that celebrity's career starts to take off, the shock may be too great. The days of leaving home unnoticed are over. Photographers will follow a celebrity anywhere, from the grocery store to a movie premiere. That's what seemed to happen to Jennifer and Cruz.

In some of the earliest interviews with Jennifer, she seemed completely devoted to her boyfreind at the time, David Cruz.

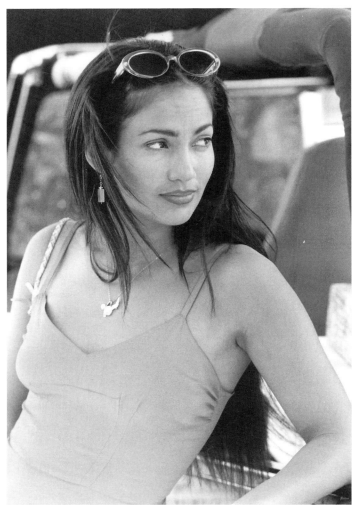

Jennifer in U-Turn

But by the time she won the lead role in *Selena*, Jennifer had already met the man she planned to marry. Jennifer first saw Ojani Noa at a restaurant owned by singer Gloria Estefan, Laros on the Beach, where he was waiting tables. For Jennifer, it was love at first sight. She supposedly told a friend, "That's the man I'm going to marry." They did start dating, and about a year later, on February 22, 1997, they were married. The marriage seemed sudden to many outsiders. Jennifer had just finished her role as Selena Quintanilla Perez and was about to begin work on two new films, *Anaconda* and *U-Turn*. But in an article in *In Style*, Jennifer seemed very much in love on her wedding day.

However, the pressures of Hollywood would hurt this marriage. As Jennifer began to win bigger and bigger roles in more popular films, the strain became obvious. They divorced within a year. She told *People*, "It's tough for me because the men I'm attracted to, for some reason, haven't gotten it together." Noa told the *New York Post*, "She wanted her career, so everything with us went out the window."

It wasn't long before she met her next love, rap star Sean "Puffy" Combs. At first, many people thought that this choice in men was another impetuous decision on her part. Jennifer revealed some of her compulsive nature when it comes to love in an article for *Vanity Fair*: "I'm an idiot when I fall in love. When I fall in love, everything else falls

The pressures of Hollywood hurt Jennifer's marriage to Ojani Noa.

Jennifer and Sean "Puffy" Combs have had a lot of attention focused on their relationship.

out the window." But she and Combs actually have more in common than many people think. They both grew up in the tougher parts of New York, they're both former dancers and entertainers (Combs is a successful hip-hop artist like Jennifer), and they're both very aggressive when it comes to success. Before getting his big break as a singer, Combs was an intern for a record company.

Combs and Jennifer, however, have not had an easy romance. They've had a lot of attention focused on them, and Combs has had more than one run-in with the law, but Jennifer stood by him. A childhood friend of Combs said, "My impression has always been that these two are genuinely in love." Even Combs himself told *Honey* magazine: "I ain't never had nobody love me the way she loves me. Hopefully one day I'll be able to marry her."

Chapter 4
Jennifer Sings

Her first love has always been dancing, but Jennifer has also always loved to sing. After the success of films like *Selena*, Jennifer was approached by record executive Jeff Ayeroff about recording a CD. Sean "Puffy" Combs, her friend at the time, also encouraged the record company to hire Jennifer. Even the head of the company, Tommy Mottola, was brought in. In the end, she signed a contract with Sony Records to record her first album, *On the 6*.

The record was named after the number of the subway train in New York that Jennifer would take from the

> **Her first love has always been dancing, but Jennifer has also always loved to sing.**

Bronx, her home, to get to the center of the city, Manhattan, where her father worked. Her drive to have a film and record career are simple, she said: "I've got to do it. I just thank God I have the opportunity."

Before her album was released, Jennifer received another lucky break— Latino singer Ricky Martin performed on the Grammy Awards show. According to *Billboard* writer John Lannert, many Latin singers owe some gratitude to Martin, whose February 24, 1999 performance on the Grammys sparked a wave of excitement nationwide for Latin music.

Although there are some Spanish-language songs on the record, including a duet with Marc Anthony, *"No Me Ames*/You Don't Love Me," Jennifer has scored her biggest hits on the album with English-language dance songs like "Waiting for Tonight," and rhythm-and-blues songs like "If You Had My Love." She had the help of several important music industry professionals like Emilio

Estefan, record producer and husband of Gloria Estefan; Rick Wake, who has worked on records for Celine Dion; and even Sean Combs.

One year after Ricky Martin's famous performance, *The 42nd Annual Grammy Award Show* featured several Latinos nominated in the Latin music categories but also in

In 1999, Jennifer won an ALMA Award, given by the National Council of La Raza.

mainstream categories like Best Song and Best Album. Latino Carlos Santana took home top honors that night for his album *Supernatural*, but Jennifer also earned some attention. Besides the sexy dress she wore, Jennifer was an award presenter at the event and she received her first Grammy nomination for Best Dance Recording for her song "Waiting for Tonight." She had already received four nominations for an MTV Video Music Award for her single "If You Had My Love."

On the 6 has been a success since its release, selling over two million copies worldwide. The first single, "If You Had My Love," stayed at the number-one spot in record sales for five weeks. Whether she continues with both her singing and acting career does not depend on how well either does, because they've both been extremely successful, but on Jennifer, and how hard she wants to continue to work. "Of all the actors and actresses who have tried to become recording artists it's hard to think of one who has done quite as well," said Geoff Mayfield, director of *Billboard*, which tracks all record sales in the recording industry.

Chapter 5
What the Future Holds

At only 30 years old (in 2000) and at the top of her form, Jennifer has a story very similar to that of many young stars. She has always known that she wanted to be a star, and she made choices, like taking dancing lessons and opting out of a college education to seek fame and fortune as an entertainer. As she continues to grow as a star, her instincts about how to market herself remain strong.

> **Jennifer has always known that she wanted to be a star.**

Jennifer had four movies released in 2000: *The Cell, The Wedding Planner, Pluto Nash* and *Angel Eyes*. She also had plans to make another record. L'Oréal

> **Jennifer remains aware of the important role she plays as a successful Latina.**

cosmetics has hired her as a spokesperson. But whatever she does, Jennifer remains aware of the important role she plays as a successful Latina. When asked by *Premiere* magazine to compare her career to the story of Cinderella or Rocky Balboa (from the Sylvester Stallone movie *Rocky*) she said, "I guess, in a way, it's a mix of both. But I don't see it [success] so much as a fairy tale as it is the result of working hard and wanting something so badly. I don't take anything for granted. I don't sleep, and I always take on more."

For director Gregory Nava, who cast her in two of his films, the importance of Jennifer's success will be felt by many future Latinos who want a career as an entertainer. "She's helping to change the industry's perception of Latinos in leading roles. Having a name like Lopez in the old days was a real disadvantage. . . . Jennifer's a great role model for our community—to say, you can achieve your dream if you have passion."

As a native of New York and a fan of actress Rita Moreno, Jennifer also hopes to be cast in an upcoming remake of the play *West Side Story.* The play was first performed in the fifties, and it tells the story of two rival gangs, the Sharks and the Jets, and how a boy and girl, whose families are members of each gang and consequently enemies, fall in love. Moreno was cast in the role of Anita, for which she won a Tony Award, the highest honor given to theater performers. For Jennifer, this would be just one other field to conquer.

She explained her ambitious nature to a reporter for *Honey* magazine: "I remember being fourteen or fifteen, and wanting so bad to be a better dancer and wanting to learn more, more, more. I remember telling my teacher, 'I just want to be better!'" In an article in *Premiere* she described her ambition this way: "I remember sitting in a movie theater so many times and seeing a trailer, like for *Terminator 2* or something, and being like, 'One day,

"I remember being fourteen or fifteen, and wanting so bad to be a better dancer and wanting to learn more, more, more," explains Jennifer.

Jennifer has become the highest paid Latina actor in Hollywood.

that's going to be me.' I had to do it, or I'd kill myself. It's that extreme."

Her ambition has produced results. She has become the highest paid Latina actor in Hollywood—she earned $9 million for her last movie. With the success of her debut album and her success in Hollywood, Jennifer will continue to excite her fans and bring pride to the Latino community.

Filmography

My Little Girl (1986)
In Living Color (1991)
Nurses on the Line: The Crash of Flight 7 (1993) (TV Movie)
Second Chances (1993) (TV movie)
My Family/Mi Familia (1995)
Money Train (1995)
Jack (1996)
Blood and Wine (1997)
Selena (1997)
Anaconda (1997)
U-Turn (1997)
Antz (1998)
Out of Sight (1998)
Pluto Nash (2000)
The Wedding Planner (2000)
The Cell (2000)
Angel Eyes (2000)

Discography

On the 6 (1999)

Chronology

- Born July 24, 1970, in the Bronx, New York
- 1975, begins taking dance lessons
- 1988, graduates from high school and decides not to go to college. Instead she lands a job in a theatrical show, *Golden Musicals of Broadway*, and tours Europe
- 1991, joins the cast of the television show *In Living Color* as a Fly Girl, part of the show's dance troupe
- 1995, director Gregory Nava casts Jennifer in *Mi Familia.*
- 1996, Nava casts Jennifer in the lead role as Selena Quintanilla Perez in his next film, *Selena*
- 1997, marries her first husband, Ojani Noa
- 1998, divorces Noa
- 1999, records her first CD, *On the 6*
- 2000, creates a sensation at the Grammy Awards with her new boyfriend Sean "Puffy" Combs

Index